Molly the Goldfish Fairy

For the fabulous Molly Shanahan,
with love

Special thanks to Narinder Dhami

ISBN-10: 0-545-04189-9
ISBN-13: 978-0-545-04189-8

12 11 10 9 8 7   11 12 13 14/0

Printed in the U.S.A.   40

First Scholastic printing, June 2008

Molly
the Goldfish
Fairy

by Daisy Meadows

LITTLE APPLE

SCHOLASTIC INC.

New York   Toronto   London   Auckland

Sydney   Mexico City   New Delhi   Hong Kong

Fairies with their pets I see
and yet no pet has chosen me!
So I will get some of my own
to share my perfect frosty home.

This spell I cast, its aim is clear:
to bring the magic pets straight here.
The Pet Fairies soon will see
their seven pets living with me!

Contents

Gnome, Sweet Gnome   1

Gnomes Alive   15

Flash Has Some Fun   27

Kirsty's Challenge   39

Tug-of-war   47

Winner Takes All   59

Gnome, Sweet Gnome

"Slow down, Dad," Kirsty Tate called. "You're leaving us behind!"

"Sorry," Mr. Tate stopped and waited for Kirsty, Rachel, and Mrs. Tate to catch up. "I'm hungry, and you know how good the Wainwrights' barbecues always are. In fact . . ." He sniffed the

air. "I think I can smell the food cooking from here!"

"We're still two blocks away!" Kirsty said, grinning and shaking her head. Her best friend, Rachel, burst out laughing.

Mr. and Mrs. Tate walked on ahead and the girls followed.

"The barbecue will be fun," Kirsty said, smiling. Rachel was staying with her over spring vacation. "The Wainwrights have a huge yard."

"Cool!" Rachel said eagerly. Then she lowered her voice. "But don't forget, we have to keep our eyes open for fairy pets, too!"

Kirsty nodded. "The fairies are depending on us," she whispered.

Rachel and Kirsty had never told anyone else their special secret. They had become friends with the fairies! Now, whenever their magical friends were in trouble, the girls always tried to help.

Jack Frost caused a lot of problems in Fairyland. This time, he had stolen the seven magic animals belonging to the Pet Fairies. But the mischievous pets had managed to escape from Jack Frost and his goblins. Now all the pets were in the human world! Rachel and Kirsty were determined to find the pets and return them to their fairy owners before the goblins could take them back to Jack Frost.

"We've found five pets so far," Kirsty went on as they turned onto the Wainwrights' street.

"Yes, we just have the goldfish and the pony left to find," Rachel said thoughtfully. "The goldfish will be tricky, though. It's the smallest pet we've had to look for!"

"Here we are," Mrs. Tate announced, opening a little white gate up ahead. "The Wainwrights said to go around to the backyard."

Rachel and Kirsty could smell the food cooking as they walked around the side of the house. It made their mouths water!

"Hello!" Mrs. Tate called as they entered the backyard. "We're here!"

A grill stood on the patio next to the house. Smoke curled

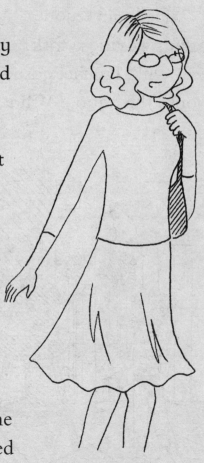

up from it as sausages sizzled. A tall man wearing a blue apron turned to grin at them all.

"Hello, everyone," Mr. Wainwright said, waving a fork.

"Oh!" Rachel gasped as she walked onto the patio. "What a beautiful yard!"

The yard was very long and wide. The emerald-green grass was dotted with bushes and colorful flowers. Stone paths wove in and out of the flowerbeds. One of them led to a large fish pond, half-hidden by weeping willow trees.

Mr. Wainwright grinned. "You must be Kirsty's friend Rachel," he said.

Rachel nodded. "Your yard is so pretty," she told him eagerly.

Mr. Wainwright looked pleased. "Thank you!" he said. "Has Kirsty told you about my prize-winning collection?"

"Your what?" Rachel asked, confused.

Kirsty laughed. "Mr. Wainwright collects garden gnomes," she explained. "There are lots of them hidden around the yard. When I was little, I used to spend ages looking for them."

"Come and see my newest addition!" Mr. Wainwright led the girls over to the picnic table and pointed at the rocks nearby. "Isn't it a beauty?"

A rosy-cheeked gnome sat at a little table among the rocks. It looked deep in thought, stroking its white beard as it stared at a tiny chessboard in front of it.

"It's so cute!" said Rachel.

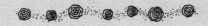

"And it looks just like Mr. Wainwright does when he's thinking!" A voice came from behind them, followed by a laugh.

The girls turned to see that Mrs. Wainwright had just come out of the kitchen. "Hello, everyone," she said, smiling. "It's nice to meet you, Rachel. I'm sure Kirsty will show you around the yard, so that you can see our other gnomes."

"Oh, yes!" Kirsty said eagerly. "I'll show Rachel the fish pond, too."

"We just bought a new goldfish named Rusty," Mr. Wainwright added. "So we have five fish now."

Mr. and Mrs. Tate began to help the Wainwrights with the food, while Kirsty led Rachel across the yard.

"Can you spot the gnomes?" Kirsty asked, pointing.

"There's one with a kite over there," Rachel laughed. "There's one on a motorcycle by the shed. Ooh, and

11

there's one in that flowerbed that's holding a tennis racket. They're everywhere!"

Kirsty nodded, grinning. "There are even more by the pond," she said, heading in that direction. "Let's go look at the fish."

Rachel followed her friend and peered into the water when they reached the pond.

"The black fish is named Shadow," Kirsty explained, "and the white one with red spots is Clown." She leaned over the water and pointed. "Can you see the red fish with white dots? That's Flame. And the little speckled one is Spots."

Rachel nodded. "That's four," she counted. Then she noticed a bright orange fish. "That must be the new fish, Rusty," she added.

Kirsty nodded, but then Rachel blinked. For a minute, she thought she'd seen a sixth fish! Rachel bent over the pool and looked more closely. There it was again: a beautiful golden fish that seemed to shimmer as it swam through the water — almost as if it was sparkling with fairy magic!

Gnomes Alive

"Kirsty!" Rachel gasped, hardly able to believe her eyes. "Did you see that?"

"What?" asked Kirsty. She'd been watching Flame and Spots, and hadn't noticed a thing.

"A sixth fish!" Rachel said, pointing.

Kirsty looked confused. "Mr. Wainwright said there were only five

fish," she murmured, frowning. But
suddenly, she spotted the golden fish,
too. Its shining tail moved gracefully in
the water.

"Look!" Rachel exclaimed. "See how
it's shimmering?"

Kirsty's eyes opened wide. The fish seemed to cast a golden light across the surface of the pond.

"Fairy magic!" Kirsty breathed excitedly. "Rachel, do you think this could be Molly the Goldfish Fairy's pet?"

Rachel nodded, grinning widely. "I'm sure it is!" she declared.

"What do we do now?" asked Kirsty, keeping a close watch on the magical fish. "Should we catch it?"

"Maybe Molly's not too far away," Rachel said, turning to look around the yard.

Just then, Kirsty saw something move out of the corner of her eye. Sitting on a rock at the side of the pond was a garden gnome, dipping a fishing net into the water. As Kirsty looked, she thought she saw the gnome's arm move. Then, to Kirsty's amazement, the gnome suddenly jumped to its feet! Kirsty blinked a few times. Was she seeing things? "Rachel," she whispered urgently. "I think the gnome by the pond is alive!"

Rachel turned to look. Sure enough, a gnome was bending over the pond, chuckling to itself. But then Rachel's heart skipped a beat. This was no ordinary garden gnome. This gnome was green all over, with a pointy nose and very big feet!

"That's not a gnome," Rachel hissed. "It's a goblin!"

Kirsty stared at the gnome and realized that her friend was right. "Oh, no!" she gasped.

So far, the goblin hadn't noticed the girls because they were half-hidden by a large bush. Rachel pulled Kirsty farther out

of sight, and then the girls peeked
between the leaves.

Suddenly, the goblin gave a gleeful
cackle. "I caught the magic goldfish!"
he called, lifting his fishing net out of
the water.

Rachel and Kirsty stared in dismay.
The goblin tipped the contents of the net
into a jar of water. The jar glowed with
golden light as the fairy pet splashed into
the water and began swimming in circles.

"Ha, ha!" the goblin chuckled, picking
up the jar and dancing
around with it. "I'm the
smartest goblin of all!
Jack Frost will be so
happy with me!"
Rachel and Kirsty
jumped as another
goblin suddenly popped
out of a bush nearby.

"Let me see the magic
goldfish!" he cried. He was
also disguised as a garden
gnome. He looked like
a golfer, carrying a
little bag of golf clubs!

"Me, too!" called
another goblin
appearing by the pond.

"Let me hold the jar!" demanded yet another.

Kirsty and Rachel could hardly believe their eyes. Goblins disguised as gnomes came running toward the pond from every direction! One had a wheelbarrow, one held a spade, and two were wearing kilts and carrying bagpipes! But they all

dropped whatever they were holding and
crowded around the jar.

"They've been hiding in the yard,
disguised as gnomes!" Rachel
whispered.

Kirsty nodded. "We have to get
Molly's goldfish back quickly," she said.
"Come on, Rachel!"

Looking determined, Rachel and Kirsty stepped out from behind the shrub.

The golfer goblin spotted them first. "It's those pesky girls again!" he shouted. "Put that goldfish back in the pond!" Kirsty said firmly, marching toward the goblins. Rachel was right behind her. "No way!" the goblin said, holding the jar behind his back and glaring at the girls. "We're taking it to Jack Frost."

"So there!" added the goblin
with the wheelbarrow.
He stuck out his tongue
at the girls, and the
other goblins roared
with laughter. Then,
before Rachel and
Kirsty could say
anything else, all the
goblins turned and ran away.

Flash Has Some Fun

"Let's follow them, Kirsty!" Rachel exclaimed.

But just then, the girls heard a tiny, silvery voice above them cry, "Wheeeee!"

Rachel and Kirsty looked up. Molly the Goldfish Fairy was swooping through the air toward them! She wore a turquoise skirt and top, and her long red curls were held back by a band of blue roses. A sparkling glass fishbowl full of water swung from her arm like a tiny handbag.

"Molly!" Kirsty said excitedly.

Molly hovered in front of the girls. "I'm so glad to see you," she declared, beaming at Rachel and Kirsty. "I have

a feeling that Flash is around here somewhere. Have you seen him?"

"The goblins captured him!" Rachel said, pointing to the very edge of the yard. The goblins were standing by the fence, arguing about how they were going to climb over it while holding the jar.

"They scooped Flash out of the pond, and now he's trapped in that jar," explained Kirsty.

To the girls' surprise, Molly laughed. "That's not a problem for Flash," she said. "Watch." She

fluttered up into the air again. "Flash!" she called. "Here, boy!"

Rachel and Kirsty saw a sparkling shimmer swirl up inside the jar. The next moment, Flash leaped out of the jar and began to swim toward them — through the air!

"That's amazing!" Rachel gasped.

"I know!" Molly laughed. "Isn't he cool? Of course, real fish have to stay in the water. But because Flash is magic, he can swim in the air, too!"

"Hey!" The goblin holding the jar

suddenly noticed that it was empty. "Where's the fish?"

"He's getting away!" another goblin shouted as he spotted Flash swimming through the air. "After him!"

The goblins chased Flash across the yard, stumbling over their feet as they ran.

The golfer goblin was faster than the

others. He caught up with Flash and
made a grab for the little goldfish.

"I've got him!" he yelled.

"No, you don't!" the other
goblins taunted, as Flash
wriggled out of the
goblin's grasp and
swam on.

"He's too
slippery," the
golfer goblin
grumbled.

"You're too
slow!" the fishing-
net goblin retorted.
"Watch *me* catch
him." He jumped into
the air and grabbed
Flash. But once

again, the goldfish slipped easily through his fingers. "You two are useless!" roared one of the other goblins. "Out of my way!" He elbowed them aside and leaped at Flash. For a moment, he held the fish in his hands. Then Flash slithered free once again. The goblin made another grab, but this time he only managed to hit himself on the nose. "Ow!" he wailed.

Rachel and Kirsty grinned at Molly, who winked. "This way, Flash!" she called, holding out the sparkling fishbowl.

Flash headed straight toward the bowl. As he swam, he magically changed in size and shape until he was fairy pet–size again. Then he swam right into his bowl.

"Good boy!" Molly cried happily.

Rachel nudged Kirsty. "What are the goblins up to now?" she whispered.

"I don't know," Kirsty replied, frowning.

The goblins were all huddled together, whispering to one another. Then, all of a sudden, they rushed toward the pond. Confused, Molly and the girls watched as the golfer goblin grabbed the fishing net. He bent over the pond, dipping the net in the water. The other goblins crowded around him.

One of the goblins took off his hat and began dipping that into the pond, too.

"What are they doing?" Kirsty asked. But then the goblin lifted his hat up out of the water and emptied it into the jar.

"Oh, no!" Kirsty gasped. A white fish with red spots tumbled out of the hat and into the jar. "They caught Clown!"

"Look, we've got this teeny-tiny fish," one of the goblins in a kilt shouted. He waved the jar at Molly and the girls. "And we're not giving it back — unless you hand over Flash!"

Kirsty's Challenge

The girls and Molly stared at one
another. Now what?

"They want us to trade Flash for
Clown!" Rachel whispered.

Flash was swimming in circles inside his
fishbowl, looking very anxious. He rose
to the surface of the water, opened his
mouth, and a stream of magical,

multicolored bubbles poured out. Molly listened closely.

"Flash wants us to hand him over," she said, biting her lip. "He says it's his job to make sure that poor Clown is safe."

"There must be another way to get back Clown," Rachel said.

Meanwhile, Kirsty was thinking hard. She knew it didn't take much to get the goblins to start arguing. All of a sudden, an idea popped into her head.

"There's another way!" Kirsty whispered excitedly. She marched over to the pond. The goblins glared at her and immediately formed a circle around the goblin with the jar.

"Look, we're all stuck," Kirsty said boldly. "You won't give up Clown —"

"No, we won't!" the goblins agreed.

"And we're not handing over Flash!" Kirsty went on firmly.

The goblins frowned.

"So let's have a competition to settle this," Kirsty said. "How about a tug-of-war? You goblins against us girls and Molly. The winning team gets both fish!"

The goblins stared uncertainly at Kirsty. Then, as she walked back to Rachel, Molly, and Flash, they began whispering again.

"A tug-of-war?" Rachel asked, looking at Kirsty in confusion. "Do you really think we can win, Kirsty?"

Kirsty nodded. "The goblins will start arguing, just like they always do," she whispered. "They won't work together as a team, so they won't win!"

Molly brightened immediately. "I like it!" she said, beaming. Flash popped up out of his fishbowl and sent a stream of  colorful bubbles toward Kirsty.

"Flash likes it, too!" Molly told her.

The golfer goblin stepped forward and scowled at Kirsty. "A tug-of-war isn't fair," he snapped. "We're all different sizes."

"No problem," Molly said breezily. "I can use my magic to make us all the same size — if you goblins will agree to

keep still, so that I can wave my wand over you."

Kirsty glanced at Rachel. They both knew that the fairies could only cast spells on goblins if they were standing completely still.

The goblins looked interested. They started whispering again. This time, they were so excited that Rachel, Kirsty, and Molly could hear what they were saying!

"It'll be five of us against three of them," the golfer goblin said confidently. "We can't lose!"

"He's right," chuckled one of the kilt-wearing goblins. "We're much stronger than a fairy and two silly girls. Let's do it!"

Tug-of-war

"We accept the challenge," the golfer goblin said, glaring at Molly and the girls. "But no tricks! You must shrink us all at exactly the same time."

"No tricks," Molly agreed. "Put the jar down on that rock."

The goblins still looked suspicious, but they did as Molly said. Molly put Flash's

bowl down on the grass,
and Flash
immediately
jumped out and
swam over near
the jar to keep
Clown company.

"Ready?" Molly
called, lifting her wand.

Kirsty looked quickly across the yard to
make sure no one was watching. She was
relieved to see that they were out of sight
of her parents and the Wainwrights.
"Ready!" she agreed, and Rachel
nodded.

"Get on with it!" the golfer goblin said
rudely.

Molly waved her wand, and a light
shower of turquoise fairy dust swirled and

sparkled around Rachel, Kirsty, and the
goblins. The two girls caught their breath
as they immediately shrank to fairy size.
The goblins shrank, too, then looked
down at themselves in disgust.

"I hate being fairy-size!" the fishing-
net goblin grumbled.

"It'll be worth it when we win," the
golfer goblin said.

In the meantime, Molly had waved her wand again. Now a long, shiny blue rope appeared on the grass. Then a sparkly line of golden glitter showed up across the middle of the rope, dividing it into two equal sections.

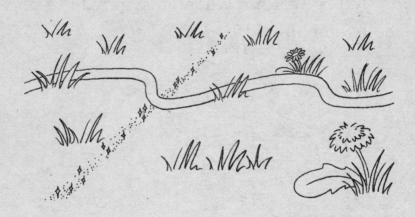

"The team that pulls the other over the line wins," Molly announced, fluttering to join the girls. "Ready?"

"No!" snapped the golfer goblin. "We have to discuss our team plan." He picked up one end of the rope. "I'm standing at the front."

The goblin who'd caught Flash tried to grab the rope. "No, I want to be at the front!" he roared.

"You should be at the back," one of the kilt-wearing goblins chimed in. "You're the biggest."

"He's the biggest goofball, you mean!" said the golfer goblin scornfully. "Now let's get on with it."

Kirsty glanced over at Rachel, trying not to smile. The goblins were arguing already, and they hadn't even started yet!

"Let's go over the rules one more time," Molly said. "Whoever wins the tug-of-war gets *both* fish." The goblins nodded impatiently. Kirsty picked up one end of the rope, and Rachel stood behind her. Then Molly waved her wand, and three fairy sparklers appeared next to the pond.

"Those sparklers tell us when to start," Molly explained. "When the third one

shoots glitter into the air, we tug!" She
put down her wand and grabbed on to
the rope behind Rachel.

"Get ready," yelled the golfer goblin,
who was at the front of his team.

Whoosh! The first sparkler
burst, sending red sparkles
everywhere. A second
later, the next one
sent out a swirl of
amber glitter.

"Get ready!"
Kirsty whispered
to Rachel and
Molly. *Whoosh!*
The third sparkler
exploded, and green
glitter flew into the air.

The girls and Molly began to pull with all their might. So did the goblins! At first, the contest was very even. Neither team could pull the other toward the line. But the goblins did have two more members on their team. At last, they began to pull Molly and the girls toward the line, a little bit at a time.

Flash looked very nervous as he swam around and around in the air. Kirsty's heart sank. She dug her heels into the grass, trying to hold on, but it was tough. She could hear Molly and Rachel panting behind her.

"We're winning!" yelled the golfer goblin gleefully. "Come on, pull harder!"

He gave the rope a huge tug. As he did, he stepped on the toe of the goblin behind him.

"Ow!" shrieked that goblin, letting go of the rope. "You clumsy fool!" He poked the golfer goblin sharply in the back.

The golfer goblin spun around, letting go of the rope, too. "Who are you calling a fool?" he snarled.

"Don't let go!" shouted the other three goblins.

"Don't tell me what to do!" yelled the golfer goblin, shoving the goblin behind him.

"Pull as hard as you can!" Kirsty whispered to Rachel and Molly, as all five goblins started snapping at one another.

The girls and Molly began to tug at the rope even harder than before. To their delight, they began dragging the arguing goblins closer and closer to the sparkling golden line!

Winner Takes All

At first, the goblins didn't even notice.

Then, suddenly, the golfer goblin gave a cry of rage. "We're losing! Pull harder!"

The goblins stopped fighting, but two of them had lost their grip on the rope. As they struggled to grab on to it again,

the girls and Molly pulled them even
closer to the line.

"You're not trying!"
yelled the golfer
goblin, who was red
in the face. He
strained at the
rope and
managed to pull
Kirsty toward
him a little. But
as he did, he
jabbed the goblin
behind him in the
ribs with his elbow.

"Aargh!" That
goblin dropped the
rope and doubled over
in pain.

"What are you doing?" shouted the one behind him. He took one hand off the rope to give him a shove. "We've got them now!" Kirsty panted. "PULL!" The golfer goblin's big green toes were almost on the line. With one mighty effort, the girls and Molly yanked him across to their side. Although they tried to dig in their heels, the other goblins came tumbling after him, one by one.

"We won!" Kirsty cried.

The goblins looked very shocked . . . and very grumpy. They instantly started arguing about which one of them was to blame.

"The contest is over!" Molly announced, picking up her wand. "Give back Clown, please."

"No!" snapped the golfer goblin.

Kirsty and Rachel looked at each other in shock.

"The contest wasn't fair!" the golfer goblin continued.

"Of course it was fair!" Rachel said.

"And you agreed to the rules!" Kirsty pointed out.

"We don't care. We're not giving back the fish!" the golfer goblin told them. The other goblins cheered.

"Well!" Molly put her hands on her hips. "I knew goblins were mean, but this is just terrible!" Then she smiled at Rachel and Kirsty. "Don't worry, girls," she whispered. "I have an idea."

With a flick of her wand, Molly sent a swirl of magic fairy dust toward Rachel and Kirsty. In the blink of an eye, the two girls were back to their normal size.

"Go and get Clown, girls," Molly said, her green eyes sparkling.

"After all, we won the contest, fair and square!"

"Hey!" shouted the golfer goblin, jumping up and down angrily. His voice was so tiny, Rachel and Kirsty could hardly hear what he was saying. "You can't do that! Stop them!" The tiny, fairy-size goblins scurried over as Rachel and Kirsty headed for the jar. But they were too small to stop the girls. Kirsty carefully tipped Clown back into the pond, and he swam away happily. Flash watched, looking pleased. Then he swam back to his fishbowl, shimmering all the way. Molly picked up the bowl, blew a kiss to Flash, and flew down to the goblins.

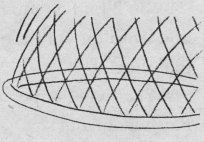

"You should have stuck to our agreement!" she said, shaking her head. She waved her wand again. Rachel and Kirsty watched as the goblin's fishing net lifted into the air and drifted toward the goblins, surrounded by sparkling magic.

The net floated down over the goblins, trapping them underneath.

"Help!" they shouted furiously. "Let us out!"

"You'll find a way to escape when you learn to work together," Molly told them.

"What will happen to them?" asked Rachel quietly.

Molly grinned. "My spell will wear off in a little while, and then the goblins will be back to their normal size again," she replied. "But by then, I will have taken Flash back to Fairyland. The other fish will be safe! And the goblins will have to hurry back to Jack Frost and tell him they've failed again."

Flash swam to the top of his fishbowl, and shiny rainbow-colored bubbles poured from his open mouth.

"Flash says thank you for all your help, girls," Molly translated, "and so do I." She glanced at the goblins, who were still arguing under the fishing net. "The goblins won't cause any more trouble today, so go and enjoy your barbecue," she said. "Good-bye!" she cried, blowing the girls a kiss as she vanished in a swirl of sparkles.

Kirsty beamed at Rachel. "Wasn't Flash sweet?" she said. "I'm so glad Molly's got him back."

"Me, too," Rachel agreed. "Now we only have one magic pet left to find. And only one more day before I have to go home!"

Kirsty nodded. "I hope we find Penny the Pony Fairy's magic pet tomorrow," she said.

67

"Girls!" Mrs. Tate called suddenly from the patio. "The food's ready."

"Great," said Kirsty eagerly. "I'm starving after that tug-of-war!"

"So am I!" Rachel laughed. "We really worked up an appetite!" The girls hurried across the yard, leaving the grumbling goblins behind.

Rachel and Kirsty have found six of the
missing fairy pets. Can they find the final
pet and help

Penny
the Pony
Fairy?

A Pony Ride

"Let's go, Jet!" Kirsty Tate shook the reins and Jet, the black pony she was riding, set off along the forest trail. Kirsty grinned over at her best friend, Rachel Walker, who was sitting on a chestnut mare named Annie. The two girls had come to Bramble Stables for an afternoon pony ride. "This is a perfect

day for riding," Kirsty said happily, feeling the warm sun on her face.

"And the perfect way to end our visit together," Rachel agreed.

The girls exchanged a secret smile.

"We still need to find Penny the Pony Fairy's pet pony," Kirsty said thoughtfully. "I really hope we can rescue her before you have to go home, Rachel."

Rachel nodded. "Well, we're definitely in the right place to spot her," she said. "This is pony heaven!"

Suddenly, Kirsty spotted a flash of green disappearing in the trees. *What's that?* she murmured to herself, peering through the leaves. But then she gasped. "Oh, Rachel, look," she whispered. "It's a goblin!"

There's Magic in Every Series!

The Rainbow Fairies

The Weather Fairies

The Jewel Fairies

The Pet Fairies

The Fun Day Fairies

The Petal Fairies

The Dance Fairies

Read them all!

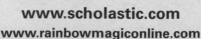

www.scholastic.com
www.rainbowmagiconline.com

RMFAIR